Your Body Belongs To You

*Many thanks to all the experts who have contributed
their opinions, advice, and kindness to this book.
Thank you to Gema Castaño, José Manuel Nava, and Susanna Isern.*

*Thank you to Romina, for giving me
the last little push I needed to complete this book.*

Lucía Serrano

Your Body Belongs To You

Copyright © 2021, NubeOcho
Copyright © 2021, Lucía Serrano (text & illustrations)
Originally published under the title "Tu cuerpo es tuyo" in Spain.
Translation arranged through MARINA Books Literary Agency, Barcelona, Spain
Translation © Cecilia Ross
This edition Mercier Press, Cork, 2025
www.mercierpress.ie

First editing: September, 2023
ISBN: 978-84-19253-71-2
Legal Deposit: M-23679-2022

All rights reserved.

Your Body Belongs To You

Lucía Serrano

Everyone has a body.
Just one.
And you can do lots
and lots of things with it.

Your body belongs to you.

And no one else.

Your body has lots of parts:

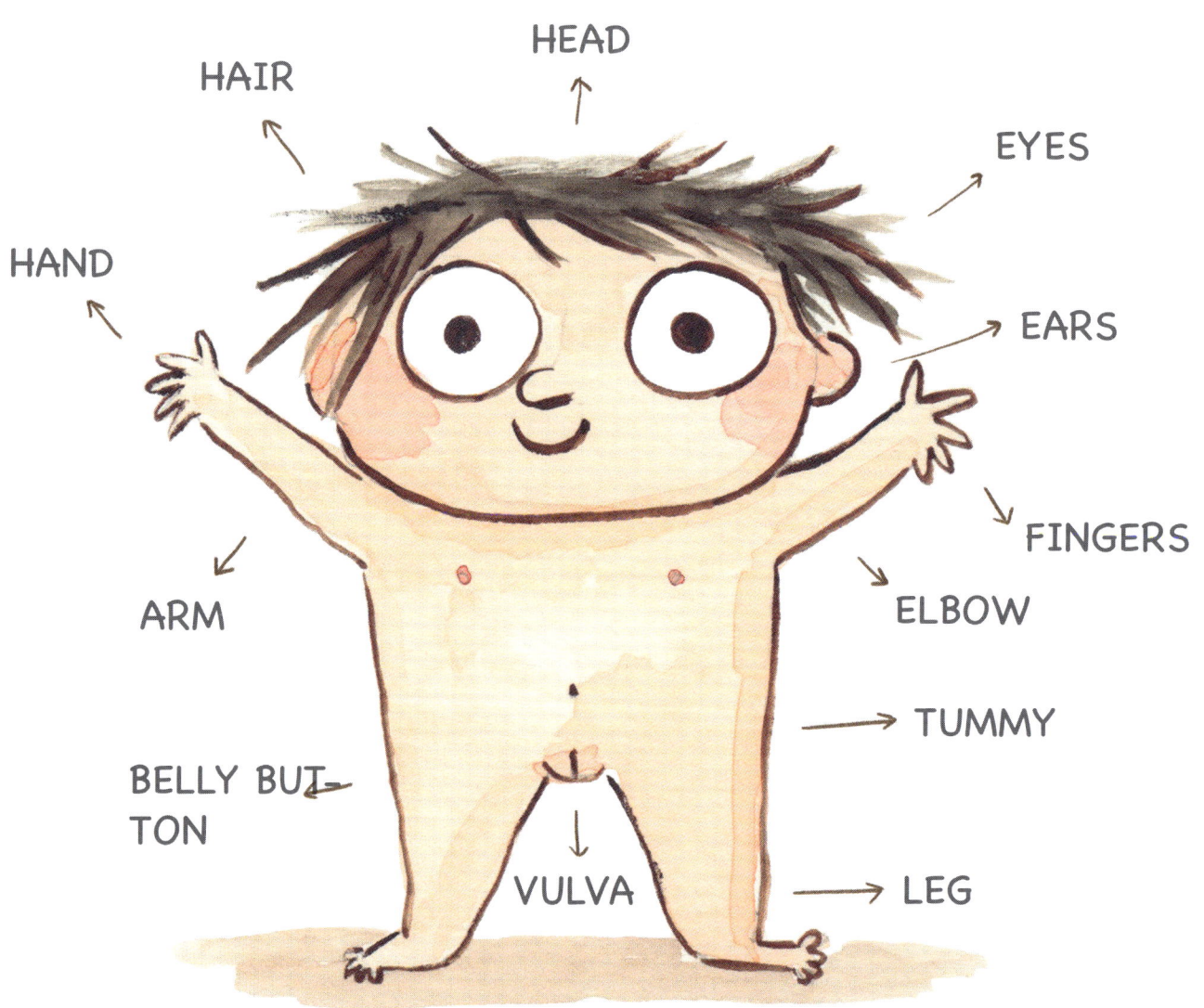

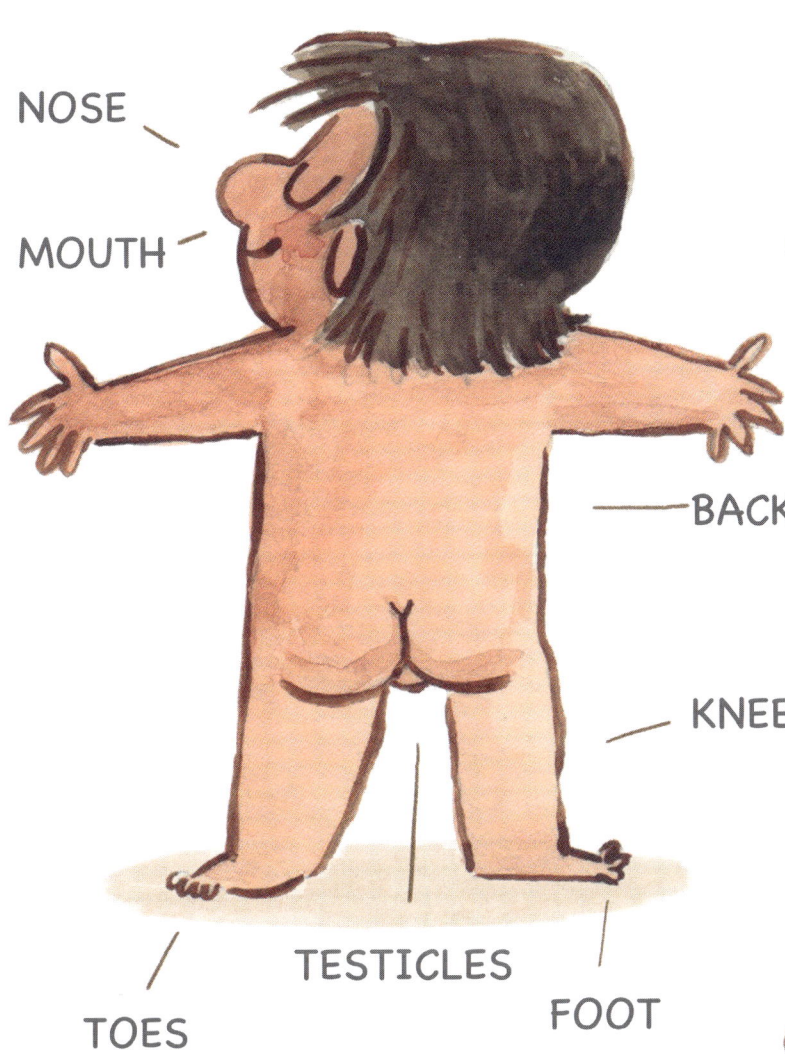

NOSE
MOUTH
BACK
KNEE
TESTICLES
FOOT
TOES

Every part of your body does something, and some parts even do several things.

And all of your body parts put together make an amazing thing: you!

Your body belongs to you, and you are the person who gets to make decisions about it.

You decide if you want someone to hug you or not.

You decide if you want someone to kiss you or not.

The word NO is a very important one. You can say NO whenever you want. Why don't you give it a try right now? See how strong you can make it sound!

When somebody else tells you not to do something to their body, you have to respect their decision. Just as they have to respect your decisions about your body.

Sometimes you might like someone to pick you up and carry you in their arms, for instance, and other times you might not. And that's just fine!

But if you're in danger, another person can touch you without asking first.

For example, if you're about to cross a busy street and a car is coming, other person doesn't have to ask your permission before they grab you to stop you.

And that's good - because they're protecting you!

Some parts of your body are private.

They're called "private parts" because those are the parts of our bodies that we usually cover with clothes and only see when we're naked.

Your private parts all have very nice names, so there's no need to use any other strange or made-up names for them.

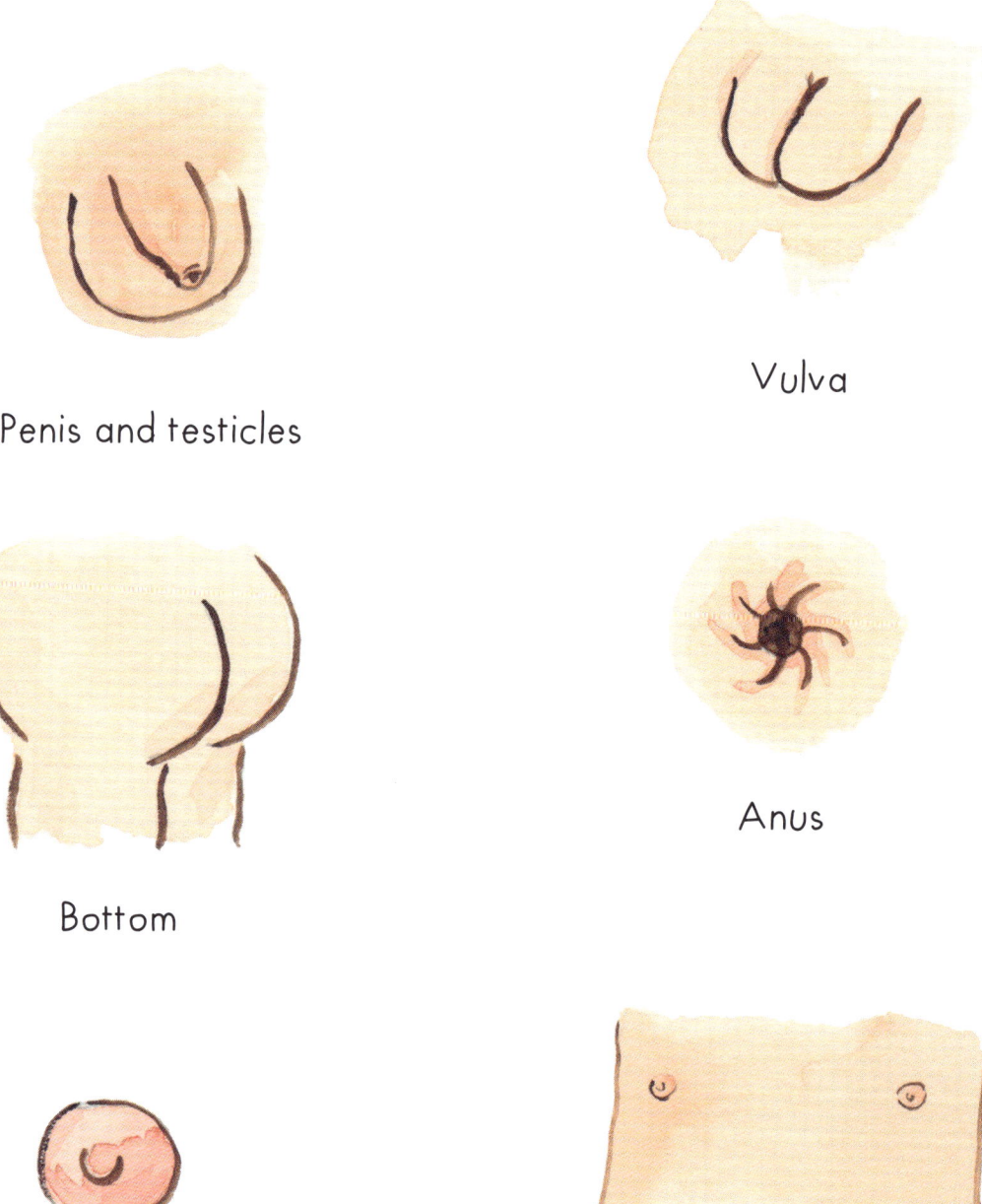

Penis and testicles

Vulva

Bottom

Anus

Nipple

Chest

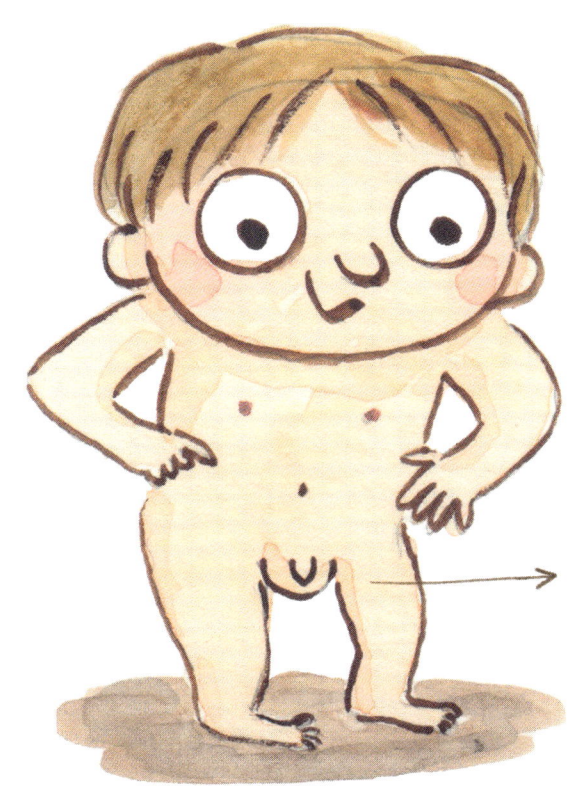

Some private parts are very easy to spot.

→ PENIS AND TESTICLES

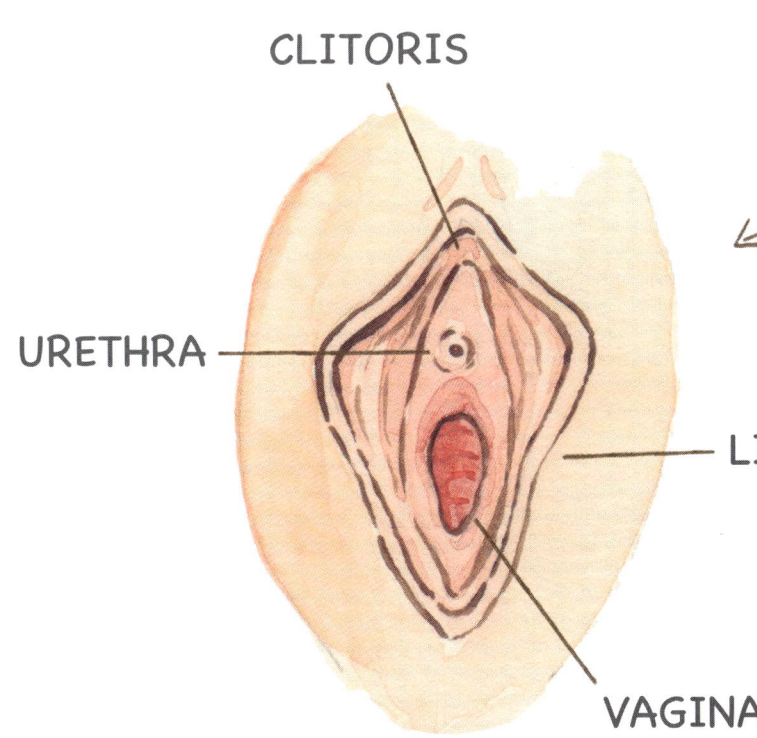

CLITORIS

URETHRA

LIPS

VAGINA

Others are more difficult to see, but you can use a mirror to help you.

Grown-ups should not touch your private parts.

So when you're taking a bath, it's best you wash those parts yourself. You have to make sure to wash them very well so that they don't get red or itchy.

But sometimes, if you're having trouble with a part of your body, you may need someone else's help. For instance, if your doctor has given specific health instructions or if your skin has become irritated. In those cases, a parent or guardian can help you.

"I need to make sure that your foreskin is healthy and that it can move properly. Will you let me touch your penis for a moment to check?"

A doctor may sometimes have to touch one of your private parts to make sure that they're healthy, or if you've gotten sick or injured in some way.

But they have to ask for your permission first and explain to you why they need to do it.

And it should always be done in the presence of the grown-up who brought you.

Something you should not do is touch the private parts of a grown-up. They're a lot different from your own private parts, aren't they?

You can ask all the questions you want about them. But you mustn´t touch them.

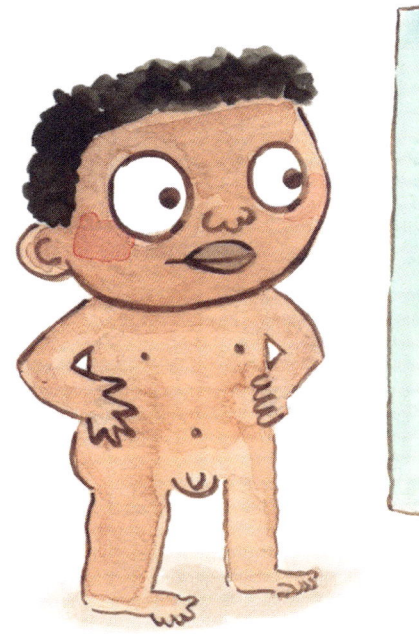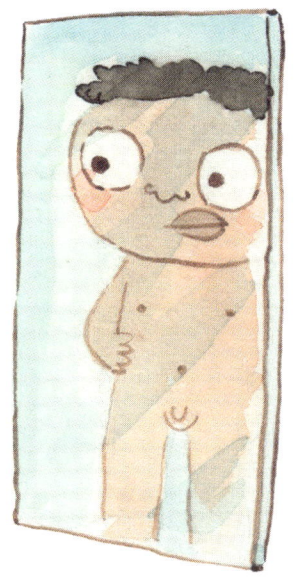

Sometimes we like to look at and explore our bodies.

This is a private activity. Sometimes we might do this with another child, but if either person feels uncomfortable about it, we have to stop.

If you tell someone "no," they have to respect your decision.

If they don't, ask someone else for help.

It's possible that a grown-up or another child could behave very badly and want to touch your private parts.

If that happens, remember - you need to go and get help.

You should never get into a car with a grown-up, or go for a walk with them, or go into their house without first telling a parent or guardian.

Parents and guardians must always know where you are.

No grown-up or other child should close the door of a room you're in together so that other people can't see you, and they must not ask you to touch their body or for you to touch your own.

If you ever feel nervous or uncomfortable in a certain room or with a certain person, you do not have to stay.

You can leave and go somewhere else.

If someone is doing something to you that you don't like, you might not be able to say "NO" - you may not be able to think clearly enough, or you might feel too nervous or ashamed to say it.

Then later, when you think about what happened, you feel upset.

Good secrets are fun, they make you smile and feel happy.
This kind of secret doesn't scare you or make you feel bad.

But if the thing you're keeping inside of you makes you feel sad or upset, then that's not a good secret.

If a secret makes you feel sad or scared, it's a bad secret.

Bad secrets should never be kept inside because they can make you feel sad, or scared, or guilty.

In fact, it's right there in their name: bad secrets make you feel bad.

When you eat something that makes you sick, your body forces it back out of you, right?

That's just what we have to do with bad secrets - get them out.

If something like this happens to you, there's a chance that the first grown-up you tell may not understand you or might not want to believe you.

If they refuse to listen to you or believe you, you'll probably feel very sad.

Then you need to keep on trying until you find a grown-up who will listen to you and believe you. It might be your mother or father, or it might be someone outside of your family. It could be a grown-up at school - a teacher, a school nurse, or the principal, for example. It could also be an aunt or uncle, a friend, or your doctor.

And you'll see that when you find someone who will really listen to you, you'll start to feel a little bit better.

Children's private parts are their own and not for others to touch.

Let's make sure everyone knows it!

A lot of people already know about the lessons in this book. They do a great job taking care of children like you every day.

You probably even know a few!

Your body belongs to you.

And your body is a wonderful thing.

And now you know a little bit more about how to take care of it and protect it!